In Every Universe, I Chose You

By Omega Mz

Shiva Desai was 42, single, and bored.

The alarm buzzed at 8:30. He groggily slid a handout from under the blanket and hit snooze without opening his eyes. Fifteen minutes later, it rang again—more insistent this time. With a quiet sigh, he pushed off the covers, silenced the alarm, and sat on the edge of the bed. A few slow stretches—shoulders, neck, arms—and then, reluctantly, he pulled himself up. Another day, another reluctant march toward the office.

His days were painfully predictable—wake up to the shrill insistence of his alarm at 8:30, scroll mindlessly through news headlines and WhatsApp forwards, then rush through a half-hearted breakfast before leaving for office by 10. Lunch was always at his desk, usually a sad sandwich, eaten while eyes flicked between emails and Excel sheets. Meetings were a theatre of hollow enthusiasm, where he perfected the art of pretend laughter and nodding at jargon-filled monologues. By 8, he was back home, slipping into his pajamas and drowning the silence with reruns on Netflix, the same shows he had watched a dozen times, not for the plot, but for the comfort of predictability.

Once upon a time, he had dreamed of being many things—a cricketer with fans chanting his name at Wankhede, a rock singer strumming chords that made people feel things, even a painter lost in a world of colour and canvas and Small family with his college time crush Sunaina who is now married as Shiva didn't had courage to express his feeling to her. But life, with its quiet compromises and unspoken pressures, had other plans. He ended up a mid-level manager at a tech firm in Mumbai, his creativity boxed into PowerPoint slides, his spirit dulled by endless traffic jams and the artificial glow of office lights. The dreams hadn't died; they had just been buried under deadlines and EMI reminders.

College had been a different universe altogether — one where time moved slower, laughter echoed louder, and friendships felt infinite.

Shiva still remembered how every day began not with alarms, but with backslaps, chai at the college tapri, and the buzz of unspoken plans. He and his gang — Raj, Namdev, Meher, Sunaina and a few more misfits who somehow fit perfectly together — made the campus feel like home. Their usual spot was the worn-out stone bench near the banyan tree, unofficially named "Adda-

101." That bench had heard everything — gossip, dreams, heartbreaks, arguments, and bursts of uncontrollable laughter that earned them disapproving looks from professors passing by.

Classes were often optional, but chai breaks were sacred. Even when they did attend lectures, they'd pass notes, doodle song lyrics, or plan which movie to catch after college. The canteen was their sanctuary — samosa pavs, cutting chai, and that one cracked table that always wobbled but never collapsed, much like their group itself.

Group studies were less about studying and more about procrastination with snacks. They'd gather at someone's house — textbooks open but mostly ignored — and dive into long conversations about life, love, Music, cricket, and the meaning of "success." Someone would always play the guitar, someone else would pretend to study, and laughter would eventually drown everything else. Nights turned into dawns without anyone noticing.

There were times they'd sneak onto the college terrace after hours — watching the city lights flicker in the distance, the stars above giving quiet company, while dreams spilled out of their hearts without hesitation. They believed they were meant for something bigger. That friendship like this would last forever. That life wouldn't change them.

College fests were the highlight — where Shiva's rock band would perform, and steal the show with his vocals. They were local celebrities for a weekend, bathed in applause and admiration. Even the failures were fun — lost matches, botched assignments, late submissions — all turned into shared jokes over late-night Maggi and bunked hostel curfews.

They didn't need much. A shared scooter, playlists burned onto scratched CDs, cheap Chinese food from the corner stall, and the promise of meeting again tomorrow. Back then, tomorrow always felt full of possibilities.

Those years weren't just about academics or achievements. They were about **belonging**. About having people who understood you without explanation. Who saw your potential when even you forgot it existed.

And as Shiva sat in the silence of his present-day apartment, those memories returned not as a pang of longing, but as a gentle reminder — of the boy who laughed without reason, who dreamt without limits, and who never imagined growing up would feel this quiet.

At present, when he was available, his friends weren't, and now that they are, the urge to reconnect has faded. That's not unusual—it often happens when we internalize unmet expectations or get used to our own company.

Sometimes, digital connection feels like enough because it's low-pressure. But if he used to value those friendships, it might help to reflect on whether this withdrawal is a form of self-protection or genuine contentment.

The same routine had played out for over a decade — like a well-rehearsed play, consistent and predictable, with the only change being the shifting dates on the calendar. The only quarterly deviation was his one-week trip to the site office in Pune, meant for process refreshers, updates, and meetings with top management.

It was a Sunday evening when Shiva packed his bag and headed to the airport. In the cab, the driver had the cricket commentary blaring from the radio — a fierce match between Mumbai and Chennai. The driver, a passionate Chennai supporter, cheered after every boundary and groaned with every dot ball. The excitement was infectious.

Shiva sat quietly, gazing out the window, but his mind wasn't on the skyline or the match. The crackle of the commentary stirred something deeper — a memory buried but never forgotten.

Back then in college time, Shiva wasn't just *in* the college cricket team — he led it. As captain of KBP College's cricket team, he was their pride. A sharp wicketkeeper-batsman with a calm head and tactical brilliance, his friends — and even some professors — fondly called him **"Dhoni of KBP."**

He had earned the name not just for his skill behind the stumps or the cool composure under pressure, but for the way he led from the front, especially in crunch situations. In the inter-collegiate tournaments, when other captains lost nerves, Shiva held his ground. Once, during a semi-final, KBP needed 28 runs off the last two overs. Most had written them off. But Shiva stayed. He scored 24 runs in those final deliveries — including two sixes that still lived in legend among his juniors.

He took the team to the finals that year. They didn't win, but it didn't matter. Shiva had become a name.

The canteen walls carried his hand-signed posters. College magazines did short interviews with him. Professors proudly mentioned him when talking about "discipline through sport." He was more than a cricketer — he was a symbol of hope for the college, a reminder that passion, if nurtured, could become identity.

But like many bright stars in youth, Shiva's cricketing journey hit a detour.

After graduation, when real life came calling — jobs, responsibilities, family expectations — cricket became a "good memory" rather than a pursuit. The bat was packed away, the shoes stored in the attic. Trials with local clubs didn't work out. One rejection turned into two, and slowly, the dream faded into routine.

Back in the cab, a wicket fell on the radio.

The commentator's voice shifted: *"And here comes MS Dhoni to the crease — the crowd erupts!"*

The driver pumped his fist, shouting, **"Come on, Dhoni!"**

Shiva chuckled quietly.

Those exact words had echoed once for him, screamed by classmates and teammates alike as he walked to the crease, helmet in hand, eyes focused. That adrenaline, that applause — it was still fresh in the corners of his memory.

A bittersweet smile curled on his lips. The past felt vivid, yet distant. Like an old photograph — edges worn, but emotions intact.

He pulled himself back to the present with a sigh, opened his laptop, and began sorting through emails. The screen glowed, full of work deadlines and meeting reminders. The match continued in the background.

Within an hour, Shiva reached the airport. His flight was scheduled from Terminal 2. After checking in his baggage and clearing security, he made his way to the boarding gate — only to hear an announcement: due to unexpected heavy rain, the flight was delayed by three hours. With no other option, he resigned himself to wait.

He placed his bag on the chair beside him and sat down, considering passing the time by watching a series on his phone. But when he reached for his earphones — checked his bag, pockets, every compartment — they were nowhere to be found. Probably left them at home, he thought with a sigh. Watching something on loudspeaker or mute didn't make sense either.

With time to spare and nothing else to do, Shiva wandered through the airport terminal, hoping a quiet stroll might ease the boredom of the delayed flight. The polished floors echoed his footsteps as he moved past cafés, travel stores, and bustling passengers. But it was the walls that caught his eye — not the usual advertisements or neon signs, but a series of hand-painted murals depicting scenes from rural India.

One particular panel made him stop in his tracks.

A traditional village scene — mud huts, bullock carts, women drawing water from a well, and children flying kites against an orange dusk sky. It wasn't just beautiful; it felt *familiar*.

A memory surfaced — vibrant, untouched by time.

He was thirteen again, standing in the corner of his classroom, brush in hand, nervously adding final touches to a painting. The school was hosting its annual art competition, and Shiva had spent days perfecting his piece: a snapshot of his grandmother's village in Konkan. He still remembered the intricate textures of the clay walls, the glint of sunlight on water, the quiet pride he took in every stroke.

When the results were announced, he had won first prize.

That moment changed everything.

His painting was featured in the school's annual magazine and proudly displayed in the principal's office for weeks. More than the prize, it was the admiration — teachers patting his back, classmates looking at him differently, his parents surprised and proud.

His drawing teacher, Mrs. Deshpande, had pulled him aside after the ceremony and said with a gentle seriousness, *"You don't just paint, Shiva. You observe. That's rare."*

She had insisted he join her weekend art class at a local studio. Hesitant at first, Shiva eventually gave in — and that studio became his sanctuary.

Hours would slip by unnoticed as he explored watercolors, charcoal, pastels. By high school, he was known as the "Local Da Vinci" — not just for his skill, but for how he breathed emotion into every canvas.

He painted everything — old temples, rain-drenched streets, portraits of his friends, even abstract emotions he couldn't put into words. Art became a language when words fell short. It gave him an identity, separate from studies, expectations, and societal boxes.

But somewhere after the 12th grade — in the tide of competitive exams, college forms, and the overwhelming call of "practicality" — the brush was set aside. The sketchbooks were stored. Not forgotten, but buried under layers of growing up.

Now, standing there at the airport, in front of that mural, those years came rushing back. The scent of turpentine. The hush of the art room. The soft scratch of graphite. The quiet pride of creation.

A gentle smile formed on his lips.

For a few moments, he let himself drift in the memory — not with regret, but with a tender acknowledgment of a version of himself still alive beneath the surface.

Then, with a calm he hadn't felt in a long time, he turned and made his way back to the boarding gate.

He didn't feel restless anymore.

He felt reminded.

After a while, a young couple arrived and took the seats directly across from Shiva. They seemed either newly married or in a fresh relationship — playful, romantic, and charmingly adorable. The boy was notably attentive, handling all the luggage, including the girl's purse. It looked a bit amusing at first, but Shiva knew — when you truly care for someone, such gestures aren't funny; they're simply part of love.

The girl was talkative, her voice animated with stories and excitement, while the boy listened intently, always responding with a gentle smile. There was no sign of irritation, no argument — just effortless joy between them. Watching them, Shiva couldn't help but think that he might've been just like that boy... if life had turned out differently — if he had ended up with Sunaina.

It had been love at first sight.

He still remembered that day — the first day of senior college. It was pouring, as Mumbai often does. He had arrived early, soaked from the rain, and used the notice board to find his classroom. The room was empty — he was 30 minutes early. Choosing the last bench in the far-left corner, he sat down and began drying his hair with his hand.

Moments later, he heard footsteps echoing in the corridor. He looked toward the door — and there she was.

The footsteps stopped, and standing in the doorway was a girl who seemed to step right out of a dream. About 5 feet 4 inches tall, fair-skinned, with deep brown eyes and long black hair. She wore a sleeveless brown high-neck dress that ended at her knees, paired with brown sandals — all drenched from the rain, clearly without an umbrella. She paused at the door, and Shiva stared, stunned. Something in his chest shifted. For the first time, he felt like his heart was melting.

Time faltered.

She stood there — in the doorway, drenched from the Mumbai rain, a moment carved out of the ordinary. Her presence didn't enter the room; it *filled* it. Brown eyes met his, and for a second, he forgot how to breathe. She wasn't just a beautiful girl in a wet brown dress. She was a moment. A pause. A possibility.

His heartbeat quickened — not with panic, but with awe. Like the first few notes of a favorite song after years of silence. He didn't know her name, didn't know anything about her. But his soul... it reacted. As if something ancient within him had finally recognized what it had always been searching for.

Her soaked sandals squeaked slightly against the floor, her eyes scanning the empty classroom — but to Shiva, she might as well have been moving in slow motion. Everything else blurred. All he could focus on was her — the gentle rise and fall of her breath, the way her hair clung to her neck, the soft vulnerability in her expression.

It wasn't just attraction. It was a sudden, overwhelming certainty: *"She matters. I don't know how or why, but she does."*

And in that fleeting moment, before a word was spoken, Shiva realized he was already falling.

Over time, Shiva and Sunaina became inseparable — best friends, confidants, partners in every college event, every joke, every secret. Their friendship was effortless, filled with shared laughter, stolen glances, and long conversations that stretched into the evening.

Sometimes, when she laughed a little longer at his jokes, or rested her head on his shoulder during college trips, Shiva felt something more — a quiet hope that maybe, just maybe, she felt the same. There were moments when her eyes lingered a bit too long, when her voice softened just for him, when she defended him like he mattered more than anyone else.

And yet, despite all those moments, Shiva never said a word.

Maybe it was fear — of ruining what they had, of losing her altogether. Maybe he kept waiting for the perfect moment, not realizing that time doesn't wait for those who hesitate. He convinced himself there would always be another day, another chance.

But the day never came.

What Shiva never knew — or maybe never dared to believe — was that Sunaina had fallen too. That very same day, on the first day of college, when she stepped into that empty classroom and saw him sitting there, drenched, slightly awkward, but with kind eyes that instantly put her heart at ease — she had felt it.

Something shifted in her too.

From that day forward, she found herself seeking him in every crowd — her eyes naturally drifting toward where he might be. She would save the seat next to her in lectures without thinking, and linger after events just to walk back with him, even if it meant taking the longer route. She laughed at his stupid jokes not out of politeness, but because they genuinely made her happy. She stood by him, always — supporting him through everything.

Every sketch he drew, every painting he made — she kept them safe, like little pieces of his soul she couldn't let go of. She cheered for him during his music performances, clapping the loudest, her eyes never leaving him on stage. And when he played his first university match, she was there too — in the stands, heart pounding with pride, believing in him when no one else did.

She listened to his silences because sometimes, they spoke louder than his words ever could.

And through it all... she waited.

She waited through every festival, every exam season, every college trip, every birthday. She waited for him to say something — *anything*.

But he never did.

And she kept giving him little signs — soft glances, heartfelt pauses, the touch of a hand that lingered just a second too long. But all she received was silence. Beautiful, painful silence.

Her parents began talking about marriage. At first, she resisted. Told them she wasn't ready. Told herself that maybe Shiva just needed a little more time.

But time, as always, was cruel.

She was forced to meet someone. A boy from a good family, stable job, polite smile. A boy who wasn't Shiva. She hoped — *prayed* — that maybe now, finally, Shiva would stop her, say the words she had waited to hear for years. That he would just look her in the eye and say, *"Don't go. Stay. With me."*

But Shiva only smiled.

And in that moment, something inside her broke.

She nodded, smiled back, and pretended. Pretended it didn't hurt. Pretended she hadn't waited all these years for someone who never came. Pretended the dream hadn't just crumbled quietly inside her.

On the day of her wedding, she kept looking at the door, half-believing he would walk in. That he would stop everything. That the silence would finally end.

But the door never opened.

And Shiva... he just kept living.

She got married. And she cried that night — not for the man she married, but for the boy who never spoke.

Shiva loved her too — more than he had ever loved anything in his life. But he kept it buried deep within, thinking that silence was safer than the risk of losing her. He mistook her warmth for kindness, her closeness for comfort, her laughter for friendship. He never dared to believe she could feel the same.

And then, one day, she mentioned her engagement — casually, as though it was just another update in their lives. Shiva smiled, nodded, even congratulated her. But inside, something shattered.

He was broken — not just by the thought of losing her, but by the belief that she had never seen him that way. He assumed she had moved on, that her heart had never been his to begin with. That their story was always meant to be one of friendship, not love. He convinced himself she was happy with the match her parents had arranged — that maybe this other man could give her the security and certainty that Shiva wasn't sure he could ever provide.

He doubted his worth, questioned his place in her life, and quietly stepped back — telling himself that if she was smiling, it meant she was content. And if she was content, then maybe... it was time to let go.

He never knew that behind her smile was a heart still waiting — for *him*.

The boarding announcement echoed through the terminal, snapping Shiva out of his thoughts like a sudden gust of wind. The memories faded, but the ache lingered — a quiet sting of heartbreak and a love that was never spoken. He stood up slowly, picked up his bag, and joined the line for boarding.

As he stepped onto the flight, a deep sigh escaped him. *"Today is one of those days,"* he thought — *a day soaked in nostalgia.* One memory after another had crept in uninvited, stirring feelings he thought were long buried. It felt like the past had followed him to the airport, sat next to him, and whispered stories he wasn't ready to hear.

With a heavy heart and a distant gaze, Shiva took his seat by the window, quietly accepting that some journeys begin long before takeoff — and some, never truly end.

The air hostess announced that boarding was complete. The last passenger to step into the aircraft was a young man — long hair flowing down to his shoulders, a guitar slung across his back, and oversized headphones wrapped around his ears. He was lost in his own world, nodding to the rhythm of a song that was loud enough for people nearby to catch snippets of the beat.

He walked casually down the aisle and, to Shiva's dismay, took the seat right next to him.

Shiva gave him a side glance and muttered to himself, *"This was the last thing I needed to see today."*

Yet again, nostalgia struck — sharp and unexpected. The young man reminded him of himself back in junior college, when he too had long hair, that same spark in the eyes, and a guitar that was more than just an instrument — it was an identity. Shiva had poured his heart into music during those years, dedicating himself to the college's *Art Circle*, a vibrant space for plays, music, and creative performances.

He had even formed a band 'MYAG Modern Young Aged Group'— had been more than a name. It was a movement. A rebellion with chords and lyrics. Formed in the charged atmosphere of the college's Art Circle, MYAG became a symbol of bold ambition and raw, unfiltered talent. Shiva and Raj were at the heart of it — two voices in perfect harmony, both literally and creatively. They wrote songs together, composed on crumpled sheets in canteens, and stayed back after lectures rehearsing until their throats went sore.

Their chemistry was undeniable. Raj's voice had a mellow depth, while Shiva's was powerful and raw. Together, they balanced fire and calm — storm and silence.

And then came *that* performance.

Queen's **"We Will Rock You"** — a bold choice. A risky one. But it paid off. The audience roared, the judges nodded in admiration, and they secured the second prize among dozens of entries.

It should have been a celebration.

But instead... it became the beginning of the end.

After the show, it was Raj who started getting noticed. Faculty members complimented his voice — "so smooth, so controlled." Peers posted clips on social media, tagging Raj with captions like *'the soul of MYAG'* and *'the real voice behind the magic.'*

And somewhere deep inside Shiva, something began to stir.

It didn't start as anger — just a quiet unease. A question whispered late at night:

"What if they think he's better than me?"

He started second-guessing Raj's ideas during rehearsals. Where once he encouraged Raj's verses, now he dismissed them. He began dominating the setlists, pushing his own solo pieces forward, undercutting Raj's contributions with excuses like, *"Let's keep the energy high"* or *"This one connects better."*

Raj noticed. At first, he kept quiet. But tension thickened like humidity in a monsoon classroom. Finally, one afternoon in the green room, just a week before another college performance, Raj confronted him.

"You've changed, Shiva," he said, placing his guitar down gently. "This band used to be *ours*. But lately, it feels like you're trying to make it just yours."

Shiva, arms crossed, voice cool and clipped, replied, "I'm trying to keep us relevant. We can't afford weak links if we want to win."

Raj blinked. "You think I'm the weak link?"

Shiva didn't answer. And silence can sometimes scream louder than words.

Raj stood there for a moment, as if waiting for Shiva to take it back. But the apology never came. The insecurity had already sunk too deep.

"I didn't think applause would make you forget the music," Raj said quietly, before picking up his guitar and walking away.

The band dissolved. Friends took sides. The Art Circle mourned the loss, but like all college stories, it faded into nostalgia, becoming another *"what could've been."*

And Shiva — he moved on. Or at least, he told himself he did.

But now, years later, sitting in a plane beside a stranger with long hair and a guitar, the memory returned like an echo. Sharp. Unforgiving. A reminder that the biggest cracks aren't formed by failure — but by pride.

He smiled, not with joy, but with a quiet ache.

Because now he knew:

He hadn't lost Raj because Raj was better. He had lost him because Shiva couldn't bear to believe someone else might shine too.

Now, watching this stranger beside him — headphones on, guitar in hand — Shiva couldn't help but smile. Not out of joy, but from a place of quiet reflection.

Every quarter, I board a flight, he thought, *but today... I've been boarding memories.*

As the air hostess began her routine safety instructions, Shiva leaned back into his seat. He closed his eyes, hoping for some rest, needing space from the emotional whirlwind this day had become.

It's like the universe is in a mischievous mood today, he mused, *unfolding page after page of a past I thought was long tucked away.*

The cabin lights dimmed, casting a soft blue glow across the aisle as the engines roared to life. Within moments, the aircraft surged forward, gathering speed down the runway. Shiva felt the familiar pressure against his chest as the plane lifted off — slicing through the night and climbing into the clouds.

Outside the window, the city lights of Mumbai blurred into a sea of gold and grey, slowly swallowed by mist and altitude. Inside, there was silence — except for the faint hum of the engine and the muffled beat leaking from the young man's headphones beside him.

As the flight stabilized, Shiva leaned back and let the vibrations of takeoff settle in his body. He wasn't afraid of flying — no, that wasn't it. But tonight, he wasn't flying through air alone. He was flying through time — soaring through old memories, past versions of himself, and paths he once dreamt of but never followed.

The quiet hum of the cabin matched the quiet ache in his chest. With eyes half-closed, he whispered to himself, almost like a confession, *"So many flights taken... yet some parts of me never landed."*

And somewhere above the clouds, Shiva surrendered — not just to the sky, but to the stories he had kept buried for far too long.

Almost thirty minutes into the flight, cruising through a blanket of clouds, something changed.

The smooth hum of the engines gave way to a sudden shudder. Shiva stirred from his light rest, sensing a shift in the air. The calm was gone — replaced by sharp jolts of turbulence that rocked the aircraft. He opened his eyes and turned toward the window.

What he saw sent a chill down his spine.

The clouds outside had darkened — not the usual grey of high-altitude storms, but an inky black mist swirling violently around the plane. Bolts of lightning cracked through the sky like veins of white fire, illuminating flashes of the aircraft's wings as they shook under pressure.

The air grew heavy, almost unnatural. Cabin lights flickered. A strange silence settled among the passengers — not panic, not screams — just a collective pause, as if something beyond understanding was unfolding.

Suddenly, a bolt of lightning, brighter and more violent than anything before, struck the wing and arced across Shiva's window.

CRACK!

A blinding flash filled his vision, and in an instant, everything went black.

No hum.

No lights.

No sound.

Just... nothing.

It felt like time had stopped.

Shiva was conscious, but weightless. No sense of motion. No feeling of being in a plane, or anywhere at all.

And then, just as suddenly — a soft glow emerged. Warm. Golden. He felt gravity again. But something was... different. He could still hear his breath, still feel the seat or may be bed underneath — but it wasn't the same.

A soft touch to his shoulder shook him gently.

Slowly, cautiously, Shiva opened his eyes.

But the hum of the aircraft was gone. No cramped seat. No seatbelt light. No fellow passengers or overhead compartments. Instead, he found himself lying on a bed — firm, comfortable, wrapped in clean white sheets. The room around him was warm and filled with color — pastel walls adorned with paintings, soft curtains fluttering against designed windows that let in the golden light of a morning sun.

He blinked, stunned, trying to steady his breath. *Where... am I?*

His eyes moved to the hand resting gently on his shoulder. Smooth, familiar.

He followed it slowly, breath held, until his gaze met the face it belonged to.

And his heart stopped.

Sunaina.

But... different.

Not the college girl in a brown dress. This was a woman — a little older, yes — but breathtaking. Her eyes still had the same depth, the same mischief. Her face was calm, graceful, confident. She looked like someone who had lived, laughed, loved.

And most unbelievably... she was smiling at him.

"You're finally awake," she said softly, brushing his hair from his forehead like it was the most natural thing in the world.

Shiva sat up slightly, his mind racing, completely disoriented. "W-What is this... where am I?"

She laughed — that same laugh, soft and musical — and said, "You fell asleep while reading again. Long meeting tomorrow. I didn't want you to wake up with a sore neck."

Her words floated in the air, unreal.

Shiva looked down at himself — he was in a simple grey T-shirt and pyjamas, his watch on the side table, a photo frame beside it. His trembling hand reached out to it.

It was a picture — *their* picture. Him and Sunaina. Smiling. Married. Holding hands.

Reality twisted gently inside him.

Is this... my life here?

A world where he *had* confessed. Where they *had* ended up together. A reality where love wasn't lost to silence, where dreams hadn't been pushed aside.

He looked back at her. She was still looking at him — lovingly, curiously — waiting for him to say something.

Shiva swallowed hard, his voice barely a whisper: "Sunaina... do I... know you?"

She tilted her head, teasing, "Well, I hope so. We've been married for seven years."

And Shiva smiled — half in awe, half in disbelief — as a tear slipped quietly down his cheek.

Sunaina looked at him, eyes gleaming with excitement.

"Get ready," she said with a smile, "today's a big day for us."

Shiva blinked, still half-lost between reality and illusion. "Big day? Why... where are we going?"

She laughed gently, a sound so familiar yet distant — like a melody from a forgotten song. "Enough of your morning jokes, dear. Today is the exhibition — *your* painting exhibition. We need to be there early, remember? To check the setup and final arrangements."

Her words hit him like a soft wave — warming yet disorienting.

My painting exhibition?

Shiva slowly swung his legs over the side of the bed, feet touching a cool wooden floor. Still unsure of what was real, he stood up and stepped out of the bedroom.

The sight before him made him pause.

A spacious, sunlit duplex bungalow — wide windows, high ceilings, warm earthy colors blended with vibrant décor. Paintings adorned the walls, some abstract, some breathtakingly detailed — all in a style he recognized.

His own.

Each corner was thoughtfully arranged, as if designed from the blueprint of his dreams. The kind of house he once sketched in the back pages of his School notebooks — *just to imagine what "success" might feel like one day.*

He stood still for a moment, overwhelmed.

Was this a dream he had somehow entered? Or... had he woken up into a life that once belonged to his deepest regrets?

Sunaina walked past him, already dressed, adjusting her earrings in the hallway mirror. "You're unusually quiet today," she said, catching his eye in the reflection. "Nervous?"

Shiva gave a faint smile. "Something like that..."

He looked around once more — at the house, at her, at the life he never lived — and decided, just for now, not to question it.

If this is a dream, he thought, *I'll live it fully. And if it's real... maybe this is the second chance I never saw coming.*

And so, without another word, Shiva turned toward the stairs, ready to get dressed — ready to step into a version of himself that had once been left behind.

Today, *his* art — and *his* love — was about to take centre stage.

By the time they reached the art gallery, the sun had climbed higher, casting a soft golden hue across the city skyline. The venue was nestled in a quiet street of South Mumbai — old British architecture blended with modern glasswork, just like Shiva had always imagined for his first exhibition. The board outside read in bold, elegant letters:

"Canvas of Time — A Solo Exhibition by Shiva Desai"

Shiva stood at the entrance for a moment, staring at the sign, his name printed proudly. Sunaina nudged him playfully, "Come on, don't get emotional now. Save that for your speech."

Inside, the gallery buzzed with quiet energy. Clean white walls bore his artworks — each one framed with precision, under soft lighting. People strolled through the aisles, murmuring praise. A few critics and art bloggers hovered near the entrance, flipping through exhibition booklets with his bio printed inside.

But Shiva wasn't looking at them.

He was staring at *his own journey* — painted across the room in oil, charcoal, acrylic, and ink.

One painting showed a rainy street, a girl standing near a college gate — her brown dress and wet sandals almost lifelike. Another depicted an empty music stage, a lone mic in spotlight — the kind he once stood before during college fests. And then there was the centerpiece — a surreal piece titled "The Flight Through Clouds" — showing an aircraft breaking through a storm.

He felt something shift inside him.

It wasn't just nostalgia — it was recognition. This world wasn't fake. It was *his,* shaped by choices he never dared to make.

As he stood before the centerpiece, an elderly man approached — dressed in a neat blazer, eyes curious and kind. "You're the artist?" he asked.

Shiva nodded.

The man smiled. "This one... it's like a metaphor for transition. From regret to redemption. Powerful."

Shiva gave a soft, thoughtful smile. "Yes... something like that."

From behind, Sunaina slipped her hand into his — a simple, grounding gesture.

For a moment, everything was still.

Shiva wasn't thinking about how he got here. He wasn't worried if this was a dream, or if he'd wake up on a plane. He only knew *this* moment was real. The applause. The art. Her hand in his.

A second chance, given not just to live — but to live *right*.

By evening, the exhibition had come to a successful close. Shiva and Sunaina, relieved and content, decided to celebrate with a romantic dinner. The soft glow of the restaurant lights reflected in their eyes as they shared quiet moments, smiles, and laughter over candlelight.

As they sipped on wine, Sunaina gently placed her hand over Shiva's and said, *"We need to leave for Delhi tonight — our next exhibition is there, and the flight's in a few hours."*

Though tired, Shiva nodded with a smile. *"No rest for the passionate, hmm?"* he teased, and she laughed softly.

After dinner, they returned home. The night was quiet, the city slowly dimming around them. They spent some intimate moments together — sharing warmth, stories, and dreams of what lay ahead.

Soon, it was time. Bags packed and hearts steady, they left for the airport, ready to take the next step in their journey.

After clearing the security check, Shiva found himself walking slowly toward the boarding gate, his steps unhurried, his mind adrift. The walls of the airport corridor were adorned with vivid murals — bursts of color and imagination painted across themes of travel, dreams, and distant skies. He paused for a moment, taking in the same images he had walked past just the day before.

And yet... something felt different.

Was it the art that had changed, or him? Perhaps it was the silence in his heart yesterday, and the quiet joy that accompanied him now.

He turned to glance at Sunaina, who was walking slightly ahead, her hair catching the soft terminal lights. She looked back at him with a gentle smile. Shiva smiled in return — a smile not of excitement, but of contentment, of knowing he wasn't alone anymore.

For the first time in a long while, he didn't check the departure screens. He didn't care whether the flight was on time or delayed. *This journey was no longer about the destination... but the company beside him.*

They reached the gate. The announcement echoed gently through the space — *"Flight to Delhi now boarding..."*

They stepped forward together, hand in hand, and soon found their seats aboard the aircraft. Sunaina slid into the window seat, her face glowing faintly in the cabin light, and Shiva settled beside her.

The final passengers boarded, the cabin doors closed, and the lights dimmed to a warm hush.

As the engines began their slow rumble, Sunaina rested her head softly on Shiva's shoulder. The rhythm of her breath against him felt like a lullaby, a quiet reassurance that everything was just as it should be.

Shiva closed his eyes.

The aircraft lifted off, carving through the night sky — not just carrying them to Delhi, but into a new chapter woven with shared dreams and silent promises.

Roughly thirty minutes into the flight, a sudden, deafening crack of lightning tore through the silence. Shiva's eyes snapped open.

The cabin was still — dim, quiet — but outside, the sky was alive with fury. Thunder rolled like ancient drums, and jagged forks of lightning lit up the heavens with terrifying clarity.

Was I dreaming? he wondered, heart pounding. He turned his head quickly — and there she was. Sunaina, safe, seated by the window, her face calm in sleep.

He let out a breath he didn't know he was holding. But just as his pulse began to settle, it happened again   —
A deeper, more violent rumble, and with it, a sight that froze the breath in his lungs.

The clouds outside had turned *black*. Not just dark — but *inked in shadows*, swirling and writhing like smoke alive with malice. Lightning slithered through them, painting the sky with veins of white fire. The plane's wings trembled under the pressure as if the air itself had turned hostile.

The atmosphere inside the cabin changed. Heavy. Pressurized. The hum of the engines seemed to fade beneath the weight of something *unnatural*.

Cabin lights flickered once... then again... And then — silence.

Not a murmur, not a rustle of panic. Just an eerie, collective stillness among the passengers. As if they, too, felt it — *Something was unfolding here... something not meant to be witnessed.*

Suddenly, a bolt of lightning — brighter, closer, almost sentient in its rage — cracked through the sky and struck the wing just outside Shiva's window.

CRACK!

A blinding white flash exploded across his vision. He threw his hand over his eyes, but the light burned   through.
And then — darkness.

Not just the absence of light...

No sound.

No motion.

No hum of engines, no pressure in his ears.

No sense of *being*.

Just a void.

A deep, endless void.

"It's happening again..." Shiva thought. Not in words — but a knowing, primal and undeniable.

He was conscious. He could feel the echo of his breath, but not his chest. Weightless. Disembodied.
Trapped in a moment that defied time.

And then... from the nothingness...

A glow.

Soft.

Golden.

It grew steadily, like a flame rekindling in the darkness.

Warmth returned to his skin. He felt the pull of gravity, the faint pressure of the seat beneath him. The stillness receded like a tide pulling away, and the light grew — not blinding, but enveloping.

The void whispered a secret it never wanted to share.

And now... he was somewhere else.

The golden glow faded slowly, like mist retreating from a rising sun.

Shiva stirred. He felt the warmth of fabric beneath him — not the stiff upholstery of an airplane seat, but the soft, lived-in comfort of a bed. His hand brushed against sheets that smelled faintly of leather and sandalwood.

His eyes blinked open.

He wasn't in a plane.

He was lying in a dimly lit bedroom — and not just any bedroom. The walls were covered with massive posters and murals of rock legends: Jimi Hendrix, Freddie Mercury, Kurt Cobain, Jim Morrison, and Lata Mangeshkar in a fusion concert pose he had *never seen before*. A glowing neon sign over the headboard read *"Live Loud, Die Real."*

Guitars — electric, acoustic, even a sitar modified with an amp cord — hung from custom racks. A vintage turntable was spinning in the corner, though no sound played. The shelves were crammed with vinyl records, old music magazines, and strange, beautiful instruments Shiva couldn't even name.

It was a dream.

Or a hallucination.

Or maybe... something else entirely.

Before he could sit up, a familiar voice broke through the silence.

"Shiva...?"

He turned quickly.

Sunaina was beside him, wrapped in a blanket, her hair slightly tousled, her expression caught between worry and wonder. *"You're awake,"* she whispered, eyes scanning his face. *"I thought... I thought you will wake up late as you hardly slept last night."*

Shiva sat up slowly, his head still reeling, the surreal textures of the room making him question reality.

"Where are we?" he asked.

Sunaina smiled, brushing a strand of hair behind her ear, and said playfully, *"So, you're still in sleep mode, hmm? We're in our bedroom, dear. Whole night you were up rehearsing and trying to memorize your speech for tonight."*

Shiva blinked, the haze still clinging to his mind. *"For tonight?"* he asked, his voice low and unsure.

Sunaina's smile softened. She stepped closer, placing a gentle hand on his shoulder. *"Yes... for tonight. The Music Awards, remember? Your song is nominated. Everyone's saying it's yours this year. But you need rest,"*

As she walked out of the room to let him rest, Shiva sat on the edge of the bed, his mind racing. The fragments of the flight... the lightning... the weightless silence... It all felt more real than a dream — more *intentional*, like a key turning inside some hidden lock of his destiny.

"Is this... another timeline? Another version of me? Or the same me... just awakened?"

He stood and walked around the room. The familiar scent of aged wood and faint cologne greeted him. The bedroom was filled with warmth, character — and unmistakable style.

The space was unmistakably *his*. A perfect blend of chaos and charm: vinyl records stacked against a reclaimed wooden wall, mood lighting, vintage rock posters, and an analog synthesizer placed reverently near the window.

He paused in front of a framed photo on the nightstand — himself and Sunaina, laughing, arms thrown around each other at what looked like a backstage party. He didn't remember that moment, but his heart recognized it.

Then his gaze drifted around the rest of the house — a grand 4 BHK duplex, sunlit through large windows, but every corner spoke *music*. Guitars lined the staircase wall. A drum kit sat behind soundproof glass. Acoustic panels, vintage mics, and an old jukebox in the hallway. Even the door handles were shaped like musical notes.

And suddenly, a memory resurfaced — sharp and vivid.

He was in junior college, sitting in a rickety café with his journal, doodling house plans. *"One day, a home filled with music. A space that sings back to me. Not just four walls — a living, breathing rhythm."*

And now... here he was.

That scribbled dream was now a living space.

Shiva ran a hand through his hair and let out a slow breath.
"Maybe... this isn't a dream. Maybe this is where all those years of longing led me. Maybe... I've stepped into the life I once only dared to imagine."

From the hallway, Sunaina's voice floated in, light and teasing.
"If you're done being existential, Rockstar, your black jacket's ready, and your stylist will be here by 5!"

Shiva chuckled under his breath and whispered, *"Alright, let's see what this version of me has to say to the world tonight."*

The day drifted by in a gentle rhythm, far from the chaos of rehearsals or the glare of stage lights.

Shiva, still wrapped in the strange wonder of this reality, stayed close to Sunaina — not out of uncertainty, but out of something deeper: *a quiet gratitude*. Every glance she threw his way, every casual touch, every shared laugh in the kitchen felt like gold dust slipping through his fingers — and he wanted to catch every speck.

He followed her into the kitchen, where the warm aroma of home-cooked food filled the space. She was humming — something soft, something familiar — and it made his chest ache in the best way.

"You never used to hover this much," she teased, chopping coriander with practiced ease. *"Maybe I've come to my senses,"* Shiva said, leaning against the counter, watching her like she was the only melody that mattered. She looked at him over her shoulder and smiled — the kind of smile that anchors a man.

They shared lunch on the balcony, their conversations light but eyes speaking volumes. Shiva didn't mention the storm, the flight, or the other timeline. Not yet. Maybe he didn't need to. This moment was enough.

Time passed like a soft ballad, and soon the clock struck five.

The doorbell rang.

Sunaina called out from the bedroom, *"That must be Vidyut — your stylist. Time to turn you into the rock god everyone's expecting tonight!"*

Shiva opened the door to find a sharply dressed man with a confident air and an armful of hangers.

"Let's make some magic," Vidyut grinned,

stepping   in.
"You're already nominated for the biggest award of the night — let's make sure you look like the future of music when you walk that carpet."

Shiva was swept into a whirlwind of wardrobe options — dark velvet jackets, silver-threaded scarves, and boots that looked like they belonged on an intergalactic stage. Eventually, they settled on a striking black ensemble — understated, elegant, but with enough edge to whisper *rockstar* without shouting.

As Vidyut did the final touches on Shiva's hair, Sunaina appeared in the doorway. She had changed into a midnight-blue gown that shimmered like stardust, her hair cascading over one shoulder.

Shiva's breath caught.

"You're staring," she said, amused.

"I know," he replied softly. *"And I plan to do it all night."*

They shared a long look — full of things not said, full of timelines converging.

Then, arm in arm, they stepped out of the house.

The car was waiting. The city lights were beginning to glow. And somewhere out there, beneath the spotlight and applause, destiny was tuning its strings.

The car rolled to a smooth halt at the grand entrance of the Auditorium, the heart of the night's biggest music celebration. The lights outside shimmered like diamonds on velvet, and the hum of anticipation vibrated in the air.

The driver stepped out swiftly and opened the rear door.

Shiva took a deep breath.

Sunaina looked at him, gave his hand a gentle squeeze, and smiled, *"Ready to meet your dream?"*

He stepped out.

The world exploded.

Camera flashes burst like fireworks. The red carpet stretched out like a royal path lined with electric energy. Both sides of the entry railings were lined with fans — hundreds of them, maybe thousands — shouting, screaming, alive with emotion.

"Shiva! Shiva! We love you!"

"Play 'Raag Shivaa!'"

"Autograph, please!"

Shiva, hand in hand with Sunaina, began to walk slowly down the carpet. Every step felt like walking into the very heart of a dream he had once scribbled on notebook pages, humming tunes in borrowed guitars during college nights.

His name roared through the air like a chant — *Shiva! Shiva!*

He smiled, dazed and dazzled, his heart thudding with a strange cocktail of joy and disbelief. He waved to the crowd, both sides, meeting eyes with strangers who somehow *knew* him. Fans stretched their hands across the railing, desperate to touch, to connect — even for a moment — with the man their hearts had already embraced.

And then came that moment — the one that didn't need music or speech.

Shiva stopped, turned to face the crowd fully, raised both hands, and bowed slightly with folded palms — humble, grounded, overwhelmed.

The cheers reached a fever pitch.

Sunaina leaned in and whispered, *"This is what you were meant for. Not just the applause — but the hearts you've touched."*

They stepped past the flashing lights and security, and entered the grand doors of the Auditorium.

The atmosphere inside shifted instantly — darker, cooler, richer. Lights danced across towering walls. A massive stage stood adorned with cosmic visuals and a shining golden mic at the center. Stars of the industry mingled, interviewed, laughed, admired.

And Shiva... had just walked into the very world that once felt galaxies away.

He looked around, still catching his breath.

"You okay?" Sunaina asked, her voice a soothing presence beside him.

He nodded slowly, smiling. *"Yeah. I think... I'm finally here."*

They made their way through the elegantly lit aisles and found their seats — front row, center — the kind reserved for those whose names were already echoing through the industry.

As Shiva settled into the plush velvet seat, taking in the grandeur of the Auditorium — the sweeping lights, the thunder of applause, the dazzling screen that bathed the crowd in a golden hue — he felt a gentle tap on his shoulder.

He turned.

Raj.

Dressed in his signature leather jacket and wearing that same crooked grin Shiva knew from their old jam sessions in cramped rooms and half-lit terraces.

Shiva stood, stunned for a moment. Then the past and present merged in a heartbeat.

They hugged — firm, real, full of a thousand unspoken memories.

Raj clapped him on the back. *"Didn't know you were this emotional, bro,"* he said with a laugh. *"But tonight... we're not just witnessing history — we're living it. We'll rock this place."*

Shiva's eyes glinted. *"Like we always dreamed,"* he whispered.

The lights dimmed. A spotlight hit the stage. And the show began.

The Music Vision Awards 2025 unfolded with rhythm and grandeur — category after category, performance after performance. The auditorium pulsed with talent, legacy, and new sounds that felt like they belonged to another realm.

Shiva watched, clapping, cheering, but part of him floated — suspended between the surreal and the real, absorbing every moment like it was his first and last.

Then, the final segment began. A hush fell. The screen behind the hosts lit up:

"Best Rock Band of the Year"

Nominees flashed across the screen — iconic names, some he'd idolized.

And then...

"The winner is... *MYAG Modern Young Aged Group!* Featuring lead singer — Shiva!"

The crowd erupted.

Raj grabbed Shiva's arm, eyes wide. *"WE DID IT!"*

Shiva stood, frozen for a second, as if his body needed time to believe. Then Sunaina rose beside him, pride shining in her eyes.

Raj gave him a playful shove. *"Go, Rockstar. The world's watching."*

Shiva walked to the stage, heart thundering. The lights, the crowd, the music — it all folded into one surreal moment as he stepped up to the mic.

Cheers faded.

A silence fell — reverent, expectant.

He looked out at the sea of faces, the lives, the energy — and then at his band, his brothers, his journey, his Sunaina.

"I once dreamed of this... in a much smaller room, with peeling paint and second-hand guitars. But the dream stayed alive — through every storm, every silence. And today... that dream has a sound, a face, and all of you."

Applause swelled like a wave.

"This award belongs to every soul who believed music could change something — even time."

He held the trophy high.

And for the first time... it didn't feel like a beginning or an end.

It felt like a return — to the self he was always meant to be.

As the applause still echoed through the grand auditorium, Shiva stepped down from the stage, the golden trophy warm in his hands, the lights above casting a soft halo around him.

The moment was surreal, electric — like walking through a dream set to the rhythm of his own heartbeat.

Then, just before he reached the aisle, a man approached him.

Calm. Smiling.

Not loud like the others. Not cheering. Just... *present*.

Shiva slowed his steps. His brows drew together.

That face.

Sharp jawline. Crisp suit. A knowing look in his eyes — one that seemed to see beyond the moment.

Shiva's breath caught.

"You... I've seen you before," he muttered under his breath.

Yes — he was the same man who had appeared after the painting exhibition — congratulating him with that same enigmatic smile.

Shiva opened his mouth to speak, confusion rising like a tide.

But before he could utter a word, Sunaina's arms wrapped around him from the side, pulling him close.

"There you are, my Rockstar!" she laughed, glowing with pride. *"Come on — the guys are waiting. It's your night!"*

Shiva blinked, half lost in the moment, half holding on to the thread of the mystery.

"Wait, just a sec—" he turned his head.

But the man was gone.

Swallowed by the sea of tuxedos and flashing lights, the crowd now buzzing with champagne laughter and congratulatory embraces.

Gone — as if he was never really *meant* to stay.

Shiva stood there for a second too long, his eyes scanning the crowd. A strange unease stirred in his chest, not fear — but *awareness*.

That man wasn't just a coincidence.

There was something more.

Something watching.

Something *orchestrating*.

Sunaina tugged gently at his hand. *"Shiva? You okay?"*

He looked at her, then at his band waving excitedly near the champagne table, then at the trophy in his hand.

He smiled — but a thought lingered like a whisper behind his eyes:

"Who is he... and why does he keep appearing in every timeline?

The celebration inside the Auditorium roared with music, laughter, and champagne toasts.

Shiva, now surrounded by his band — his brothers in sound — was pulled into the rhythm of the moment. They clinked glasses, posed for photos, shouted over the music, and reminisced over how far they'd come. Raj threw his arm around Shiva's shoulder and shouted, *"From Canteen jams to global stages, baby!"*

But even in the noise, something tugged at the edges of Shiva's mind — a quiet thread of unease.

By 10 PM, the glittering celebration began to wind down. Shiva and Sunaina slipped out through a side exit, fingers intertwined, laughter still on their lips.

Their car cut through the sleeping city, neon lights flickering on tinted windows. When they reached home — their musically adorned duplex that still felt like a dream — Shiva felt that strange longing again.

They changed into something comfortable. The house was quiet. Safe.

He held her close as they sat on the edge of the bed, her head resting on his shoulder.

Sunaina reminded him about the next show in Bangalore and had to leave tonight. And that's when it hit him — not the fear of losing success, but the fear of losing *her*.

"Sunaina," he said softly, almost hesitantly, *"do we really have to go to Bangalore tonight?"*

She looked up at him, puzzled. *"Of course. The next show is one of our biggest... Are you feeling okay?"*

Shiva paused, choosing his words carefully.

"I just... I don't want this night to end. Being here, with you — like this — I don't want it to slip away. What if we... took a break? Skipped this one?"

Her brows furrowed. *"Shiva... we can't. Not now. Cancelling the show at this point would send the wrong signal — to the media, to the fans. It's not just about us anymore."*

He lowered his gaze.

"It's not about the fans, or the fame. It's..."

But he didn't finish.

Because how could he explain it?

How could he tell her he feared that stepping onto that flight might tear him from this reality — from *her* — again? That each time he soared into the clouds, he risked losing the one constant in all the chaos?

She cupped his face gently. *"You're tired. You've been through a lot lately — maybe the pressure is catching up. Let's get through this show. Then we'll take a break. Just the two of us. I promise."*

He gave a weak smile and nodded, but inside, the storm had already begun.

They packed in silence, soft music playing in the background — an acoustic version of one of Shiva's early songs. Nostalgic. Melancholic.

At midnight, the car arrived.

Their bags were loaded. The house lights dimmed.

Hand in hand, Shiva and Sunaina stepped out once more — into the night, into the unknown.

As the city disappeared behind them, and the airport lights came into view, Shiva tightened his grip on her hand.

He looked at her, memorizing every detail of her face.

"If this is a dream," he thought, *"let it be the one I never wake up from."*

But the boarding gate awaited.

And the sky — restless, waiting — held secrets yet to unfold.

After the security check, Shiva and Sunaina made their way toward the boarding gate.

The airport buzzed with its usual midnight rhythm — rolling luggage wheels, soft announcements, flickering flight status screens. But to Shiva, it all felt distant... muffled... like background noise in a dream that was slowly fading at the edges.

He was still holding her hand.

Tightly.

Sunaina glanced at him, a hint of surprise flickering in her eyes. She smiled softly but didn't say anything — sensing something, perhaps, but not yet knowing *what*.

Shiva wasn't ready to tell her.

Not yet.

Not that he was scared.

Not that every boarding gate now felt like a threshold to a new reality.

He prayed — not aloud, not in words — but in the way his heartbeat against his chest. That *this* would be the last time. That *this* version of life... this love... would hold.

But deep inside, he knew.

It won't stop here.

The boarding announcement echoed across the terminal, and they stood. Shiva took a deep breath as they walked toward the gate, passing the same uniformed ground staff, the same calm nods, the same smiling faces that seemed far too familiar.

The aircraft door welcomed them with a polite *"Good evening"* — and a strange déjà vu that chilled his spine.

They found their seats.

Sunaina by the window.Shiva next to her.

Just like before.

And then...

There she was — the same airhostess, standing at the aisle, beginning the safety demonstration with the same gestures, same cadence, same practiced grace. He stared at her, heart beginning to pound.

"It's her again. Every time."

He turned slightly in his seat, trying to scan the rest of the crew.

Yes — they looked familiar. Too familiar. Like background actors cast in multiple roles across different plays.

Passengers? Not the same. He noticed no one from the earlier flights.

one memory flickered — the guy with the oversized headphones and the worn guitar case. Not here as well.

"What if I flew a different airline?"

"What if I just... never boarded again?"

The plane began to taxi.

His thoughts swirled. *Maybe if I choose differently, I can break this loop... or at least, control where I land...*

Sunaina gently rested her head on his shoulder, eyes closed, calm as ever.

Cabin lights dimmed.

Outside, the runway glowed in fleeting yellow strips, growing faster with every second.

Shiva exhaled.

He closed his eyes — but didn't sleep.

He surrendered — not to peace, but to inevitability.

And just as the nose of the aircraft lifted from the ground, Shiva's thoughts whispered:

"If this is fate... then where is it taking me next?"

Darkness settled.

The plane disappeared into the clouds.

A low growl of thunder stirred Shiva from his half-conscious daze.

His eyes fluttered open.

Outside, the world had turned nightmarish.

Not just dark — black, like the sky had been drowned in ink. Clouds churned and twisted, alive with something far beyond weather.

Lightning sliced through them like serpents of pure energy, painting the heavens with jagged, fleeting veins of white fire.

The plane shuddered — a metallic tremble that vibrated through the cabin walls, through Shiva's bones.

The air inside thickened, heavy with pressure. Breathing felt... deliberate. Forced. The mechanical hum of the engines seemed to drift away, replaced by a looming silence that pressed against the skin.

Cabin lights flickered once.

Then again.

Then—
Stillness.

Not a cough. Not a whisper.

The passengers around him sat like statues — wide-eyed, still, as though they, too, sensed it.

Something was happening.

Something *not meant to be seen.*

As if the veil of this world was about to lift.

Shiva's hand tightened around Sunaina's, but she didn't stir. Her head still rested gently on his shoulder, serene... unaware.

And then it struck.

A blinding bolt — brighter than anything yet, like the sky itself had split open with rage — tore down and struck the wing just outside his window.

CRACK!

A white flash exploded in his vision.

Everything vanished.

No sound.

No motion.

No light.

Just... void.

And in that silence, that awful silence, Shiva closed his eyes.

He didn't fight it.

He didn't scream.

He simply *yielded* — to the inevitable pull of the unknown.

And that same familiar sensation returned:

Weightlessness.
As if he was no longer bound by physics or flesh.
As if the universe itself was folding around him.

He drifted.

He waited.

For the next door to open.

For the next world to call his name.

And just before the light came again, one last thought passed through his mind — clear, sharp, unshakable:

"Who am I, really, in all of this?"

A gentle tap on his shoulder stirred Shiva from his daze.

He blinked.

Gone were the aircraft walls, the thunderclouds, the soft cabin lights.

Instead — cheers. Thunderous, deafening. The scent of sweat, turf, and adrenaline thick in the air.

He was sitting in a cricket pavilion.

The roar of a packed stadium surged beyond the glass. The air was electric with victory.

Standing beside him was none other than Greatest Cricket Player Dhoni, his jersey streaked with grass and pride, grinning like a schoolboy.

"Stop praying, Captain," Dhoni laughed, his hand still on Shiva's shoulder. "Come on! Let's go out there and grab that trophy. We made history, man!"

Captain?

Shiva glanced down.

There it was — the navy-blue Indian jersey, his name SHIVA emblazoned on the back, the tricolour arm band tight around his bicep. His fingers trembled slightly, the weight of it all slowly settling in.

We won.

India had won the World Cup.

And he — Shiva — was the captain who led them there.

He rose to his feet, his heartbeat syncing with the rhythm of a billion cheers.

As he stepped out onto the field, a tidal wave of sound exploded from the stands.

"SHIVA! SHIVA! SHIVA!"

Confetti rained. Flags waved. The crowd became a blur of colour and emotion, of history unfolding in real time.

Cameras zoomed in. Commentators shouted his name. Teammates waited at the stage, their eyes shining with triumph.

But Shiva... Shiva was looking for something else.

Someone else.

His eyes scanned the stadium — the VIP box above the crowd — and there she was.

Sunaina.

Elegant. Composed. Proud.

She stood among dignitaries and celebrities, but her gaze was only on him. She blew him a flying kiss, her smile wide and glowing, eyes shimmering with joy.

And in that instant, the world faded again — not into blackness, but into something golden.

Shiva's chest swelled.

He stepped up, accepted the glittering World Cup Trophy, and held it high above his head. His teammates surrounded him, arms raised, shouting, laughing, crying.

They lifted him on their shoulders, and he let them — waving to the crowd, heart thundering with joy and disbelief.

And as they ran a celebratory lap around the field, flags in hand, fireworks painting the sky, one thought shimmered through Shiva's mind—

In every world, I rise... but only when she's there.

The grand ballroom of the seven-star hotel shimmered in opulence. Chandeliers sparkled overhead, the floor buzzed with the hum of celebration. Celebrities, cricketing legends, business tycoons — all were gathered to honor the man of the hour: Shiva, the World Cup-winning captain of India.

Dressed in a tailored navy tuxedo, Shiva stood with Sunaina at his side — radiant in a gold-embroidered saree — as waves of congratulations flowed toward them.

Every handshake, every compliment echoed with the same word: *"Proud."*

But Shiva's heart was only half present. Somewhere beneath the laughter and the applause, a familiar unease churned within him — the quiet pull of something unresolved.

Then it happened.

Out of the crowd, moving silently like a shadow slipping through light, the man appeared. He looked the same — always the same — across realities. Simple attire. Serene eyes. Ageless face.

He stepped beside Shiva and offered a calm, deliberate nod.

"Congratulations, Shiva. You did well."

Shiva turned sharply, his heart thudding.

"Do you know... about all this? What's happening to me?" Shiva asked, voice low and urgent.

The man smiled faintly.

"Maybe."

Then, just like that, he turned and walked toward the exit.

Shiva took a step forward, instinctively reaching out — but his teammates swarmed him, tossing him on their shoulders once again. The music roared, the celebration resumed.

By the time Shiva freed himself and made his way out, the ballroom had faded into silence behind him. He followed a stone path into the tangent garden, a beautifully lit space with gentle fountains, swaying palms, and a hushed breeze.

There, on a bench beneath a lantern's glow, the man sat quietly — waiting.

Shiva approached, cautious but determined, and sat beside him.

"I want to know. Everything. What's happening to me?"

The man didn't look at him, just stared out at the reflecting pool ahead, his voice calm as ripples.

"Our universe... is not the only universe, Shiva. Instead, there could be many — maybe even an infinite number — coexisting beyond the veil of what we consider reality."

Shiva's breath caught. "Parallel Universes."

The man turned now, meeting Shiva's eyes for the first time with a knowing smile.

"Exactly. Every choice you make... every quantum possibility, every flicker of thought... it splits. Time fractures. Realities branch. In one universe, a door opens. In another, it doesn't. In one, you turned back. In another, you walked forward."

He continued, voice smooth like a teacher, or perhaps... a guide.

"In one life, you spoke to Sunaina — you told her what you felt. And she stayed. That decision alone opened timelines where you thrived: as a painter... a rockstar... a cricketer. In each, she walks with you, because you made the right move at the right moment."

Shiva was silent, absorbing it.

"And the failed ones?" he finally asked. "What about them?"

The man looked out again.

"They're there. Real. Some where you gave up. Some where fear won. Some... where you didn't survive. Each shaped by a version of *you* who made a different choice."

A hush settled over them, heavy with truth.

Shiva stared at the stars above the garden, the weight of infinite lives pressing gently on his shoulders.

"So... what now? Will I keep jumping?"

The man stood up slowly, dusting off his hands. His voice held a note of finality.

"That depends. Some journeys are meant to show you your power, your truth. Others... are meant to bring you home."

Shiva looked up and then looked at man and asked. "Who are you? Are you a God."

The man's smile lingered like a forgotten song, almost wistful — as if he carried a thousand unspoken truths in the curve of his lips. He turned, stepped into the shadows of the garden path, and began to fade... dissolving into the night like mist in moonlight.

Just then, Sunaina's hand gently touched Shiva's shoulder.

He turned — surprised, yet somehow expecting her.

"What are you doing here?" she asked, her voice soft, grounding him. "Come on… let's go inside. They're all waiting."

Shiva took one last glance over his shoulder.

The man was gone.

Together, hand in hand, they walked back into the golden-lit ballroom, rejoining the celebration. Music soared, champagne sparkled in glasses, laughter danced in the air. Shiva smiled, not just for the applause, but for the quiet truth that lived in his chest — she was here, again… always.

It was nearly midnight when they left the celebration and returned to their home — a bungalow draped in cricketing glory. Trophies, jerseys, bats with signatures, and framed newspaper headlines adorned the walls. A world crafted around a man who had led his nation to glory.

But tonight, it felt like a sanctuary, not a shrine.

They changed into comfortable clothes and entered the bedroom, where warm light fell across the space like a lullaby.

Sunaina slipped into bed beside him, snuggling close.

"I hope you remember..." she began, her eyes teasing.

Shiva interrupted, half-laughing, half-anxious. "Wait — are we going somewhere? Do we need to catch a flight?"

She chuckled and kissed his forehead. "No, my overthinking husband. You promised me — after the final, you'd take a month off. Just us. You, me, time. And nothing else."

A sigh of relief poured out of Shiva's chest, and he wrapped his arms around her tightly.

"I'm not going anywhere now, Sunaina. I promise. I love you."

"I love you too, Shiva. Always."

They kissed, gently, as if sealing a vow across realities. Time slowed. For once, he didn't want to chase answers — only hold on to this moment, this peace. Together, they drifted into sleep, their fingers still intertwined.

CRACK.

A subtle jolt. Not violent. Just enough to break the fabric of a dream.

Shiva's eyes snapped open.

Overhead, he heard a voice.

"Ladies and gentlemen, welcome to Pune International Airport."

Confused, Shiva looked around.

He was seated on a plane.

A commercial flight.

Passengers stirred as the aircraft taxied. He turned to his side — a man wearing oversized headphones and a travel pillow sat next to him, dozing peacefully.

He scanned the cabin.

The same air hostess walked past with her routine smile. Same crew. Same ambiance. No thunder. No flickering lights. No Sunaina.

Just... the flight.

Shiva's heart raced.

Was it all a dream?

Or... another jump?

Then, the cockpit door opened. The pilot stepped out to greet the passengers before disembarkation. Friendly, calm, professional.

Shiva froze.

It was him — the same man, the one who'd met him in every timeline.

The man looked at him.

Their eyes locked.

He smiled — not broadly, but with that same subtle, eternal knowing.

Then he walked past Shiva, down the aisle... and vanished into the crowd, leaving behind only a trail of questions and one impossible truth:

It was real. All of it.

Shiva sat back in his seat.

The world outside the window was the same.

But he was not.

A week later, Shiva boarded his flight back to Mumbai.

The airport bustled with life as usual — trolley wheels clattered, announcements echoed in loops, and coffee cups steamed in strangers' hands. But for Shiva, everything moved a beat slower, like the world had softened its pace to let him catch up.

As the engines roared and the seatbelt sign blinked above his head, he rested his back and closed his eyes.

Just before takeoff, he whispered to the skies —

"Just one more jump... just one glimpse of Sunaina again."

But the skies stayed still.

No lightning split the heavens.

No inky clouds swirled.

No mysterious smiles waiting on the other side of turbulence.

Just the ordinary hum of a life moving forward.

When he stepped into his apartment that night, it felt smaller somehow. Not in size — but in sound. In silence. In presence. As if the walls themselves were exhaling after holding their breath for too long.

It wasn't empty.

It was waiting.

Shiva dropped his bag and walked to the window. The city lights blinked below like forgotten stars. He sat on the floor, pulled out an old sketchbook — untouched for years — and flipped it open. The pages were yellowed, corners curled, dust nestled like time's signature.

He picked up a pencil and let his hand move — without reason, without perfection.

Faces appeared.

Moments.
Versions of Sunaina — smiling beneath stadium lights, swaying to music, standing beside his canvas.

It wasn't sadness. It was reverence. A quiet honouring of the love he found again and again.

The next morning, he rummaged through the attic and found his old guitar — strings rusted, wood dull with age. He cleaned it gently, like an old friend returned from war. He tuned it, struck a chord, and though it wasn't perfect, it rang true enough to wake something in his chest.

By the weekend, he picked up the phone.

He called Raj.

There was a pause. A long one.

Then — laughter. And warmth. And forgiveness.

They met for chai at their old spot, like nothing and everything had changed.

That Sunday, Shiva walked into a local cricket coaching centre.

No press.

No crowd.

No trophies.

Just kids in white kits, a dusty pitch, and the distant thump of leather meeting bat.

He didn't go there to lead.

Or prove.

Or win.

He just played.

Felt the sun on his back.

Felt the earth beneath his feet.

Felt alive.

He didn't need to be a rockstar.

He didn't need to be a painter or a cricketing legend.

He didn't need the applause, the lights, the headlines.

He only needed the fragments — the brushstroke, the chord, the swing — reminders that those dreams weren't lost.

They were his.

And slowly, the truth began to settle deep within him — like mist lifting from a valley.

The multiverse hadn't shown him what he missed.
It had shown him what was still possible.

And maybe the most extraordinary life wasn't out there in some parallel plane —

But right here, in the moments he could shape with his own hands.

The life he could still choose to build.

Not for glory.

Not for destiny.

But for love.

For meaning.

For peace.

A single life.

His own.

Epilogue

It was a quiet Tuesday morning when Shiva found himself wandering through the tangled lanes of Bandra, guided by nothing but a need for stillness.

The city was just beginning to stir — the chaiwalas heating their first brew, the breeze smelling faintly of the sea and yesterday's rain. Somewhere distant, a bell rang in a temple.

He wasn't searching for anything. Not really. Maybe just a little silence. Maybe to step out of his own   thoughts.
Maybe... to lose himself in someone else's story for a while.

Tucked into a narrow by lane that time seemed to have forgotten, he spotted the old bookstore. It was still there. Its wooden sign faded, almost illegible, like a secret meant only for those who truly needed to find it.

Shiva stepped inside. The scent hit him instantly —Paper, ink, dust, and memories.

It was the kind of place where time didn't pass, it curled up in corners and waited.

He drifted between shelves, brushing his fingers over spines like old friends. The classics section called to him — not because he was looking for a classic, but because the worn and frayed felt familiar.

Then, without warning, a book dislodged from the top shelf and tumbled to the floor.

A small thud. Nothing dramatic. But when Shiva looked down, his breath caught.

The title read: "Timelines and Tethers: Love Across Universes."

He smiled. A slow, quiet smile. A coincidence? Or maybe... not.

He crouched down and picked it up. The cover was soft with age, the corners rounded, the pages whispering stories long read and often returned to.

As he opened it, a folded piece of paper fluttered out from somewhere near the middle. It drifted down like a feather, landing on the toe of his shoe.

He froze. Something about it felt intimate, fragile — like a memory trying to find its way back.

He bent, picked it up, and slowly unfolded it.

The handwriting was unmistakable.

Elegant. Slanted. Familiar. His heart skipped.

"Dear Shiva, I don't know which version of me you will meet next — or if you will at all.

But if you're reading this, it means the universe was kind enough to leave a breadcrumb for you.

Maybe we were artists.

Maybe we sang.

Maybe we played under stadium lights.

Or maybe... we just passed each other in a crowded street and never spoke.

But know this — In every universe where I could choose,

I chose you.

– Sunaina"

Shiva didn't move for a long time.

The note trembled between his fingers, and something inside him — tightly coiled, gently aching — unwound.

No thunder cracked.

No lightning struck.

No strange portals opened.

Just the whisper of ceiling fans overhead...
And a heart, slowly stitching itself back together.

Outside, the sky had cleared. The sunlight spilled
in through the open doorway, warm and golden
like memory made real.

He closed the book, pressing the note gently
between its pages once more. He didn't need to
keep it. He had already carried it with him all
along.

Before leaving, he placed the book back where it
belonged. Not because he didn't want it —

but because someone else might one day need
to find it too.

He stepped out of the shop, letting the soft air fill
his lungs.

And for the first time in what felt like lifetimes,
he smiled toward the sun.

Because somewhere — across stars, across
songs, across decisions and dreams —

love had never left.

It had only taken the long way home.